W9-BYB-717

Come on home, dog.
Come on, let's run.

All right, I give up.

You like me, don't you, you old dog?
Well, I like you, too.

Why don't you go away?

Don't look so sad, dog.
Don't look that way at me.
Can I help it if you don't have a home?

But I have to go home now.
No, you can't come.
Go away now, dog.

That was fun, dog.
Maybe we can play again.

You can run fast all right.

All right, let's run, dog.
Can you run as fast as I can?

If I play with you, will you go away?

I didn't say to lick my hand.
Stop that, you old dog.

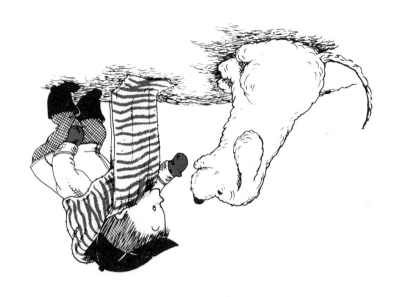

Can you shake hands?
This is how to shake hands.

Say, do that again.
Roll over again, dog.
Say, that's not bad.

You aren't bad for a dog.
But I don't like dogs.

Don't wag your tail at me.
I don't like dogs.

Don't you have a home?
Well, that's too bad.
But you can't come home with me.

Go away, you old dog.
Go on home now.

Don't jump on me, dog.
I don't like that.

If I throw it again,
will you go away?

What do you want now?

There now, go away with your stick.

If I throw the stick,
will you go away?

I don't want that stick.
Don't give it to me.

I don't like dogs at all.
Big dogs, little dogs.
Any dogs at all.

Go away, you bad old dog.
Go away from me.
I don't like you, dog.

by JOAN L. NØDSET

Away, Dog

pictures by Crosby Bonsall

📖 HarperCollins*Publishers*

GO AWAY, DOG
Text copyright © 1963 by Joan L. Nødset
Text copyright renewed 1991 by Joan M. Lexau
Illustrations copyright © 1963 by Crosby Newell Bonsall
Illustrations copyright renewed 1991 by Crosby Newell Bonsall
Printed in the United States of America. All rights reserved.
Library of Congress Catalog Card Number: 63-11162
ISBN 0-06-024555-7
ISBN 0-06-024556-5 (lib. bdg.)

For Aslang Nødset